EXACTLY ALIKE

Written and Illustrated

by

Evaline Ness

EXACTLY ALIKE

CHARLES SCRIBNER'S SONS, NEW YORK

IN an old dingy house next to a railroad track, there once lived a girl named Elizabeth. Although she herself was quite ordinary, Elizabeth had an extraordinary problem—four freckled brothers who all looked exactly alike.

BENNY   BERTIE

BUZZIE and BIFF

They made Elizabeth miserable. They pulled her hair and pinched her arms. They blew their whistles in her face. Whooping and crowing, they beat their drums and galloped about like a herd of horses. One broke her doll, one hid her skates, one always untied her hair ribbon. And one liked to jump from the closet and scare her.

Which of the four could Elizabeth blame? She could never tell who was who. When she thought one was Benny, he'd say he was Bertie. Then Bertie would say he was Biff or Buzzie. No matter how much Elizabeth begged, not one of the four would tell her his name.

IT was no use complaining to her mother. Her mother was too busy. Every day she sat at the sewing machine stitching satin gowns and velvet coats, skirts and capes of silver and gold, for the ladies of the town. All day long the sewing machine whirred and twirled, never stopping long enough for her mother to listen.

IF the sewing machine did stop, the train raced by – hissing, chuffing, clicking, clacking, shaking the house all over. Furniture trembled and dishes rattled. Pictures fell from the walls. Sometimes the windowpanes cracked. When that happened, Benny, Bertie, Buzzie and Biff bellowed louder than ever – and Elizabeth ran to her room.

Hidden under her bed was a palace which Elizabeth had made from a sewing basket. The palace had two rooms, both carpeted with red velvet. All the walls were hung with silk and satin draperies. In one room the King and Queen sat proudly on their thrones. They rarely talked. In the other room lived the Princess with her horse William. William was snow white with a perfect black star in the middle of his forehead. His tail was long and silky. His manner was dignified. He and the Princess had long conversations with Elizabeth about her extraordinary problem. William called it a mystery.

There is a clue to every mystery," William said. "Find the clue and you solve the mystery. No two living things are exactly alike, not even the leaves on a tree. So stop complaining, Elizabeth. Close your mouth and open your eyes and look."

The Princess always gave the same advice. "Leave home and never come back," she would say imperiously.

Elizabeth thought that was a marvelous idea, but she had no other place to go. So she promised William she would close her mouth and open her eyes and look.

E very day Elizabeth looked at Benny, Bertie, Buzzie and Biff.

SHE looked at their feet when they hopped and ran. She watched their hands when they ate. If they opened their mouths to yell or yawn, Elizabeth inspected their teeth and tongues. She peered at their noses, necks and arms; at their eyes, ears, lips and legs. She examined their chins, their shins and knees. She looked at every hair on their heads.

And soon Elizabeth began to *see*.

She saw four clues—one for each brother. First she found a small freckle out of place, right on the tip of a nose. Then she discovered one blue eye—all the others were black. Next she spied a tiny dimple in the middle of a chin. And last, Elizabeth noticed two slightly pointed ears which made her think of a fox.

William was extremely pleased with Elizabeth. He called her a clever girl and said he was glad her mystery was solved. Now they could talk about something other than her extraordinary problem.

At first Elizabeth was pleased too. She called her brothers Freckle Nose, Fox Ears, Blue Eye and Dimple. She always surprised them by knowing exactly who did what. But whenever she asked for their own real names, they blew their horns or beat their drums louder than ever before.

Elizabeth began to worry again.

She decided she still had a problem in spite of what William thought.

One night she said, "I think the names Benny, Bertie, Buzzie and Biff are much nicer than Freckle Nose, Fox Ears, Blue Eye and Dimple. I do wish I knew which name was which."

"Oh, why bother with names," snorted William. "Give and take a name, what does it matter? It's who you are, not what you're called. But if you insist on names, why not call them all one. Something like Berbuzzniff or Beebersnuff, or other."

"Give and take," murmured Elizabeth. "Did you say 'give and take'?"

"Why don't you leave home and never come back?" asked the Princess.

But Elizabeth knew now that she didn't want to leave home. She wanted to solve her problem and William had given her an idea.

GIVE and take. Give and take." She tried to sort it out, but she was too sleepy. Too sleepy even to put the palace back under her bed.

When Elizabeth opened her eyes the next morning, she was horrified to see Benny, Bertie, Buzzie and Biff playing with her palace. Screaming, she leaped from her bed and pushed them away.

Then she remembered: "Give and take."

Suddenly she smiled at her brothers. She took the King, the Queen, the Princess and William from the palace and held them out to the boys.

"If I give you my most precious things, will you give me back your very own names?" asked Elizabeth.

Benny, Bertie, Buzzie and Biff gazed longingly at the King, the Queen, the Princess and William. They looked at Elizabeth. They looked at each other. Then all four stuck out their jaws and slowly shook their heads—no.

Elizabeth's smile faded. She looked down at William and stroked his long silky tail. At last, blinking back the tears which filled her eyes, she said, "Well, take them anyway. Knowing you're each different is more important to me than knowing your names, I guess."

Benny, Bertie, Buzzie and Biff took their gifts.

W ithout a word of thanks they marched from the room.

Elizabeth went to her palace. She removed the red velvet carpets from the floors and the silk and satin curtains from the walls. Then she turned the palace upside down and sat on it.

SHE thought about "give and take."

Something was wrong. She had treated it like "give and get." She realized now that "give" meant *giving,* without asking for something in return as she had done. And "take" really meant to *accept.* Accept something *given.*

"Oh, dear," Elizabeth sighed. "I understand it all now, but it does make me feel dizzy."

At that moment she heard snickery snorts that sounded like water running out of a bathtub. Elizabeth opened the door.

There stood Benny, Bertie, Buzzie and Biff, holding two drums, a whistle and a horn. They gave them to Elizabeth.

Elizabeth stared at her brothers.

All at once and all together they began to talk and giggle. At first Elizabeth couldn't understand a word they were saying. But little by little and bit by bit, this is what she heard: A present for Elizabeth from

BennyFreckleNose   BertieFoxEars   BuzzieBlueEye   BiffDimple.

They were telling Elizabeth their own names at last. *They* understood "give and take" too!

Just then the train roared by, clicking, clacking, hissing, chuffing, shaking the house all over. Benny, Bertie, Buzzie and Biff bellowed with delight.

Elizabeth beat the drums and blew the whistle and the horn.

Then all at once and all together, all of them hugged each other.